"L et's see, who should I invite?"
Nathan wondered as he sat at the dining
room table. He was so intent on a list of names in
front of him he didn't even notice his sister, Anna,
walk in.

"What are you doing?" she asked as she put
her book bag down on a chair.

"Oh, I'm trying to decide who to invite to our birthday party," replied Nathan. (Nathan and Anna were twins and always had their birthday parties together.) "I want to invite only the best people."

"What do you mean, 'the best people'?" asked Anna.

"Well, you know. The ones . . . like us."

Anna thought for a moment. "How about Shannon? She's new at school, but she's nice."

"Shannon? I don't know, Anna. I heard her say on the bus that her family doesn't even go to church!"

"But, Nathan, that's no reason to—"

The conversation was cut short by someone hollering "Help!" The voice came from the backyard amid the rustle and crunch of branches. "Help me!"

Nathan and Anna jumped up from the table and dashed through the house to the backyard. There was Uncle Alphonso dangling from a tree by the garage. He clutched a rope attached to an enormous balloon that was caught in the topmost branches of the tree. "Don't just stand there!" he sputtered. "Get the trampoline!"

In a minute the children dashed outside rolling a little, round trampoline. They got it in place just in time. A quick drop and a few large bounces brought the old man safely back to earth.

"Are you all right, Uncle Alph?" asked Anna anxiously.

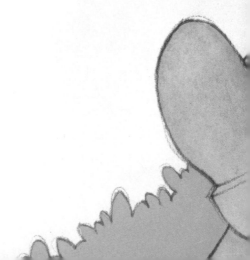

"All right? I'm terrific! It works! I knew it!"
Uncle Alphonso was giggling and dancing
around the yard.

"W-what works?" asked Nathan.

"What? Why, my experiment, of course.
Haven't I told you about it? It's one of the
biggest breakthroughs of my career!

"Another giant step forward for
Boneheadology!"

(Uncle Alphonso was a famous fossil expert
and was always having career breakthroughs.
He had a way of finding fossils no one else had
even heard of! He called them the Boneheads.)

"Sounds good, Uncle Alph," said Nathan. "You've discovered a new type of dinosaur, right?"

"Right you are, Nathan. One of the boneheadedest, too!"

"But what does that have to do with you being stuck in a tree holding a big balloon?" asked Anna.

"Everything, my dear girl," replied her great-uncle earnestly. "Come with me. I'll show you!"

Uncle Alphonso lived just down the street.
Nathan and Anna were always eager to see his
fossil collection, so off they went.

As the twins approached Uncle Alphonso's house from the alley, their eyes grew wider and wider. From the clothesline in the backyard fluttered several enormous pairs of colorful swimming trunks. Each pair was ripped up the back!

Nathan ran over to look at them more closely. "Where did you get these, Uncle Alph? No one on earth wears a swimsuit this big!"

"Not anymore, Nathan, but they used to," replied Uncle Alphonso excitedly. "These are exact replicas*—er, copies, you know—of trunks I found on my last dinosaur dig. They were worn by my newest dinosaur discovery."

"Why did you make . . . rep-lickers?" asked Anna.

*rep-li-ca

"Replicas? Oh, I had to, Anna. The originals were too fragile. I used these copies to test my theory about how these creatures died out."

"Well, how did they?" asked Nathan.

Uncle Alphonso squatted down and motioned for the children to come closer. Then he whispered, "They got too big for their britches!"

"What do you mean, Uncle Alph?" asked Anna.

"I mean they thought they were better than others. That's why I call this creature the Bigobritchosaurus.*

*big-o-**britch**-o-sau-rus

"They were seagoing dinosaurs, you see. They lived in the shallow water around islands and were the first to wear swimsuits. Green with pink sea horses, mostly. They were so proud of their suits, they began puffing themselves up to show off. They finally became the bossiest, snootiest creatures in the whole sea.

"It seems that one day the Bigobritchosauruses were having a puffing-up

contest. There they were, all floating in a lagoon with their noses in the air. They were puffing up as never before. The puffier they got, the tighter their suits stretched until—"

"R-r-r-rip!" Nathan supplied the sound. "Their suits split right up the back!"

"Bravo, Nathan!" exclaimed Uncle Alph. "That's my theory, anyway."

Anna's eyes lit up. "So that's why you made these—what did you call them—replicas?"

"Right! I wanted to see how much hot-air pressure it must have taken to split the suits."

"But what happened?" Anna asked. "Did one of the Bigobritchosauruses win the contest?"

"No, Anna. I'm afraid they all lost. They were too proud to quit puffing, so the contest continued. Before you could say 'Bigobritchosaurus,' they had all puffed

themselves up so big they began floating off into the sky.”

"The first hot-air balloons!” squealed Anna.

"So that's what you were doing with the balloon!” said Nathan with a clap of his hands.

"Exactly," replied Uncle Alphonso. "Research, my boy!" Then he added with a sigh, "But as for the Bigobritchosauruses, the wind carried them all off and they were never seen again."

Nathan decided to try on a pair of giant swim trunks. Anna and Uncle Alphonso laughed as his muffled voice came from within the colorful heap of cloth. "I think I see why those things died out, Uncle Alph. They didn't seem very smart."

"Oh, it had nothing to do with being smart or not," chuckled the old scientist. "The real problem was pride, Nathan. And I'm afraid it didn't die out with the Bigobritchosauruses!"

"What's pride, Uncle Alph?" asked Anna.

"Pride? Why, that's easy. It's . . . uh, . . . well, it means . . ."

"Being puffy?"

"Yes, Nathan. That's right. Being puffy. Acting too big for our britches."

"Like thinking we're the best people and not including others?" said Anna quietly.

"Yes, yes. Quite right."

"Like thinking someone's not good enough to invite to our birthday party?" added Nathan, glancing at his sister.

"You've got it!" exclaimed Uncle Alph. "Now there's pride if I ever saw it. I tell you, you kids understand these things better than I do myself!"

"It sounds like pride can hurt people," remarked Nathan after a pause.

"Oh, it does, Nathan," replied Uncle Alphonso, "but that's not all. Thinking we're better than others makes God sad, and it hurts us, too. It separates us from other people and takes away the joy of following Jesus."

Just then, a girl about Nathan's and Anna's age came riding by on a bicycle. She slowed to a stop when she saw Uncle Alphonso and the kids talking in the yard. "Hey, what's going on here? You guys having a party or something?"

"Hi, Shannon," replied Nathan. "No, we're not having a party." Then he paused for just a moment before adding, "But Anna and I are having our big birthday party next Wednesday. You want to come?"

Shannon seemed truly surprised. "Y-you mean it? Sure, I'll come! It sounds like fun!" The girl hopped on her bike and sped off down the street.

Just before she disappeared around the corner, she called over her shoulder, "Thanks, you guys!"

Nathan was just turning and saying, "You'll come, too, won't you, Uncle Alph?" when he stopped short. The children looked up, their eyes wide as dinner plates.

There was Uncle Alphonso holding his balloon
and floating off over the house!

"What's that? Come to your party? I'd be
delighted!" he shouted. "And don't worry. I'll
bring the balloons!

"Hel-l-lp!"